Spotter's Guide to
THE
WEATHER

Francis Wilson, F.R.Met.Soc.
and Felicity Mansfield

Special Consultant:
Harold Gibson
National Weather Service, New York

Illustrated by Ralph Stobart

Photography by Ken Pilsbury, F.R.P.S.

Contents

Editorial Director

Sue Jacquemier

Designer

Bob Scott

Additional photographs lent by
Robin Stockdale, Dundee
University Electronics
Laboratory and the Controller of
Her Majesty's Stationery Office

First published in 1979 by Usborne Publishing
Limited, Usborne House, 83-85 Saffron Hill,
London EC1N 8RT

Printed in Great Britain.

How to use this book

This book is a general introduction to the weather. It deals first of all with the three basic elements that cause all weather: the energy of the sun and the atmosphere, and water on the earth. Then it explains how these elements combine to produce different kinds of clouds, winds, precipitation and storms – everything from dew to tornadoes.

Forecasting

The section on pages 48 to 54 describes how the weather can be forecast. People use information collected from many sources, including satellites, computers and weather stations.

You may like to set up a weather station at home or at school so you can make your own weather reports and forecasts. The section beginning on page 55 tells you how to use and make simple weather recording instruments. By entering your observations in a log book, you will build up a picture of the general weather patterns in your area, and will soon be able to tell if it's going to be foggy, sunny or rainy, without relying on the official weather forecasts.

Glossary and index

There may be a few words you don't understand. Some of them are explained in the short glossaries in the colored strips across the top of various pages. Others are explained in the text. You can look them all up in the index at the back of the book.

Clouds

There are some photographs and descriptions of all the main types of clouds on pages 14 to 22. Whenever you see a cloud, try to identify it, then put a check in the small blank circle next to the right photograph. Sooner or later you should see most of the clouds listed, wherever you live.

Check off each type of cloud when you have seen it

Atmosphere and pressure

> **Atmosphere** – air. A mixture of nitrogen, oxygen, carbon dioxide, small amounts of other gases and some water vapor.
> **Water vapor** – water in gas form. Tiny, invisible particles (molecules) of water, suspended in the atmosphere.

The earth is enveloped in a blanket of atmosphere hundreds of miles thick, held down to the surface of the earth by the force of gravity. Heat from the sun stirs up the atmosphere and keeps it moving. The most changeable layer, where weather frequently happens, is the lower six miles or so, called the troposphere.

The troposphere is the only layer that has enough water vapor to form clouds. Without water vapor, there would be no rain, snow, hail or dew – no weather, in fact. Above the troposphere is a calmer layer, called the stratosphere. The boundary between them is known as the tropopause.

Each square yard of the earth's surface has about 22,000 pounds of air above it. The weight of air on a certain area exerts a force – air pressure – which is measured with barometers.

As you go higher up, the air becomes less dense and air pressure falls. This is because there is less air above you. Airplanes have to be specially pressurized because they fly at altitudes where the air is too thin for people to breathe.

Air pressure is exerted in all directions. Air inside your body presses outwards and helps keep the pressure of the air around you from squashing you flat.

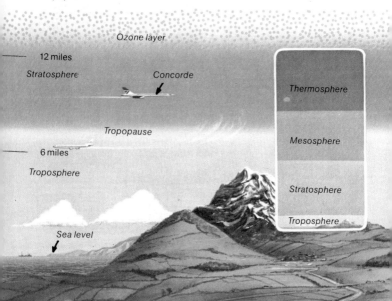

Ozone layer
12 miles
Stratosphere
Concorde
Thermosphere
Tropopause
Mesosphere
6 miles
Troposphere
Stratosphere
Troposphere
Sea level

Here is a simple experiment you can do to demonstrate air pressure. First, fill a bowl with water. Then hold an empty glass under the water until all the air inside it bubbles out and it fills up with water. Turn the glass upside down and lift it up until its rim is just below the surface of the water in the bowl. The pressure of air on the surface of the water in the bowl will stop the water in the glass from falling out.

At sea level, air pressure is strong enough to hold up a column of water over 30 feet high, or a column of mercury (the heaviest known liquid) about 30 inches high. Mercury barometers work on this principle. They are glass tubes containing mercury, and are marked off in inches or millimeters.

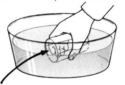

Make sure there's no air left in the glass

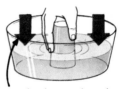

Air pressing down on the surface of the water

Aneroid barometers measure air pressure. The scale is marked off in inches (or sometimes millimeters or millibars), equivalent to the height of a column of mercury in a glass tube. At sea level, average air pressure is about 29.92 inches, 760 milimeters, or 1013 millibars.

An aneroid barometer is a metal box, partly emptied of air so that it forms a partial vacuum. When air pressure rises, the box contracts; when it falls, the box expands. As the sides of the box move in and out, a needle attached to it moves and points to a dial marked in inches or millibars.

Some barometer dials are also labeled "Rain", "Fair" and so on. These labels are not important. It is important to notice whether pressure is rising or falling, however. A rise in pressure may mean settled weather ahead, and a fall, unsettled weather.

▲ **An aneroid barometer (millibars)**

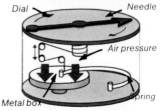

▲ **Diagram of an aneroid barometer**

Radiation

Radiation - energy in the form of waves (light and heat).

The earth's heat and light come from the sun, a huge star made of tremendously hot gases, 93 million miles away. The sun radiates enormous amounts of energy, but only a tiny proportion of it ever reaches the earth.

Energy waves from the sun travel through the atmosphere, without warming it, and are absorbed by the earth. Dark surfaces, like plowed soil, absorb more radiation than bright or polished surfaces, like snow, which reflect it. The earth warms it up and gives out the energy it receives, as heat. This warms the air.

Some of the earth's heat escapes into space, but a lot is trapped and reflected back by water vapor, carbon dioxide and clouds in the atmosphere, which absorb heat well. In the end, the earth loses about the same amount of heat as it gains, so its overall temperature is fairly even. (The moon has no atmosphere to retain heat, so its temperature drops to −220°F when it's in shade.)

Because the sun is very hot, it gives out short wavelength, intense rays. The earth is much cooler than the sun; it gives out longer wavelength, weaker rays.

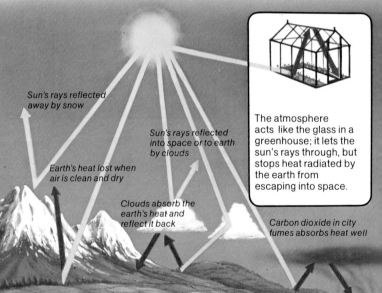

Sun's rays reflected away by snow

Sun's rays reflected into space or to earth by clouds

Earth's heat lost when air is clean and dry

Clouds absorb the earth's heat and reflect it back

The atmosphere acts like the glass in a greenhouse; it lets the sun's rays through, but stops heat radiated by the earth from escaping into space.

Carbon dioxide in city fumes absorbs heat well

Shortwave radiation from the sun
Longwave radiation from the earth

Here are some examples of different kinds of radiation:

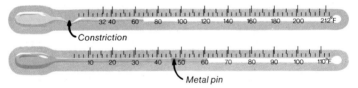

Ultraviolet light –
Short wavelength, harmful energy, given out by the sun. Ozone layer (in the stratosphere) protects us by absorbing most of it. Invisible to us.

Visible light –
Sunlight. The most important radiation we get from the sun. Longer wavelength. It looks white, but is all the colors of the rainbow.

Infrared light
The heat given out by the earth. Even longer wavelength. It can be photographed by special cameras, but we can't see it.

Because the surface of the earth is curved, the sun's rays strike it at different angles. The Equator is the hottest part of the earth, because the sun's rays strike it directly, in an almost straight line. The North and South Poles are the coldest places, because the sun's rays strike them at a very slanting angle and are therefore spread out over a wide area.

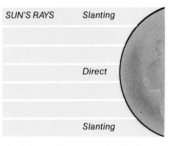

SUN'S RAYS   Slanting

Direct

Slanting

▼ **Maximum thermometer (above) and minimum thermometer (below)**

Constriction

Metal pin

Temperature is measured with thermometers. Maximum/minimum thermometers record the highest and lowest temperatures reached in a certain period.

The maximum thermometer contains mercury. When the temperature rises, the mercury expands and rises in the tube. When it stops expanding, it stays at the highest level it reached. A constriction (a very narrow passage) near the bulb of the tube stops it from running back down.

The minimum thermometer contains alcohol. When the temperature falls, the alcohol contracts and drops, carrying a metal pin down the tube. The pin stays at the lowest level reached by the alcohol when it expands again.

Sunlight

▲ A red sunset sky

▲ A double rainbow

We can only see the colors in a ray of sunlight when the ray is bent and split up, by a prism or by something blocking its path. The main colors in sunlight are red, orange, yellow, green, blue and violet. Each color is a slightly different wavelength; red is the longest wavelength, and blue and violet the shortest.

When a ray of sunlight comes across an air molecule, its colors bend. The shortest wavelength colors are bent most. Our eyes pick up the blue and violet, bent towards us from air molecules all over the sky. (The sky looks blue because we can't see violet as well as we see blue.)

When the sun is setting, its rays have to travel a long way before they reach us. They meet so many air molecules and bits of dust in the sky that all the shorter wavelength colors are bent and scattered away. When you look straight at a sunset, the sun and the sky around it look red. The sky away from the sun may still look blue. It is lit up by indirect rays that still have some blue and violet in them.

Raindrops can act as prisms. When a ray of sunlight shines on a raindrop, it bends and splits up into all its colors. The colors are reflected off the back of the drop and come out, bending once more. The colors bent by a shower of raindrops form a circle, which you could see from an airplane; from the ground, you see a semicircle – a rainbow. You can only see a rainbow if the sun is fairly low in the sky, and you are standing with your back to the sun, with the rain shower in front of you.

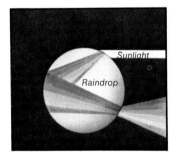

The colors go from red on the outside of the rainbow to violet on the inside. If the rays are reflected twice inside the drops, a second, fainter rainbow, with the colors in reverse order, appears around the first one.

Water in the atmosphere

Condensation – this is what happens when water vapor changes into liquid water.
Evaporation – this is what happens when liquid water changes into water vapor.

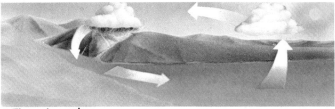

▲ The water cycle

Water exists in the atmosphere in three forms: water vapor, liquid water drops (in clouds, fog and rain) and ice (in very cold clouds, as ice crystals, hailstones and snowflakes). Water changes from one form to another by evaporation, condensation, freezing and melting.

Water covers 70 percent of the earth's surface. It evaporates out of seas, lakes and oceans into the air above. When the air is cooled low enough, the water vapor it contains condenses out, making tiny drops of liquid water. Fog and clouds are made of these drops, and so is the mist your breath makes in cold weather. The water drops in clouds turn into rain and snow and fall to earth again. Rain and melted snow collect in streams, which flow into rivers. The rivers flow back to the seas, lakes and oceans, and the water cycle begins again.

Huge quantities of heat are involved every time water changes form. It takes a lot of heat to boil water and make it evaporate, or to melt ice into liquid water. You feel cooler when you sweat because water in your skin is using heat from your body to evaporate into the air. This heat is called latent heat. It is released back into the atmosphere during freezing and condensation.

Sublimation is a special change water can make when the temperature is below freezing ($-32°F$). This means that water vapor freezes straight into ice crystals, or ice evaporates straight into water vapor, without first changing into liquid water.

▲ Boiling water evaporates from the kettle into the air. When the air cools, its water vapor condenses out, making steam.

9

Fog, dew, frost and rime

▲ When warm air flows over cold seas, its water vapor condenses out and makes **sea fog.**

▲ **Morning fog** – caused by cold mountain air blowing downhill; it soon evaporates in the sunshine.

▲ The ground cools fast on clear nights; the water vapor in the chilled air above condenses as **dew.**

▲ **Frost** – on freezing nights, dew and water vapor form ice crystal patterns on windows.

▲ **Frost** can form on the ground if dew freezes – and if water vapor in the air sublimates.

▲ **Rime** – the very cold water drops in freezing fog coat whatever they touch in a crust of ice crystals.

Humidity

> **Humidity** – the amount of water vapor in the air. When the air is warm and moist, it feels sticky. We say it's humid.

Humidity depends mainly on the temperature of the air. Warm air can hold more water vapor than cold air. For example, a cubic yard of air with a temperature of 86°F can absorb up to 0.8 ounce of water vapor while a cubic yard of air at a temperature of 50°F can only absorb a third of an ounce.

When air has absorbed as much as it can, at its temperature, it is saturated. Unsaturated air can go on absorbing water vapor, because it contains less than the maximum amount possible.

When saturated air is cooled, it can no longer hold as much water vapor; some of it has to condense out. The temperature at which condensation happens is known as the dew point of the air.

Relative humidity is the amount of water vapor actually in the air, compared to the amount it would contain if saturated. It can be measured with hygrometers.

The hygrometer consists of two thermometers called the dry and wet bulb. The dry bulb thermometer records the temperature

of the air. The wet bulb thermometer usually records a lower temperature; the bulb is wrapped in wet muslin, and water evaporating from the muslin cools the bulb. By using tables called hygrometric tables, you can convert the difference between the two readings into a percentage figure; this figure is the relative humidity. When both readings are the same, the air is saturated; the relative humidity is then 100 percent. The greater the difference in the readings, the drier the air is, and the lower the relative humidity is. Relative humidity of about 50 percent is quite comfortable to live in.

▼ **A wet and dry bulb hygrometer**

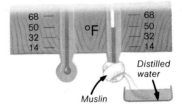

Distilled water

Muslin

		DIFFERENCE BETWEEN THERMOMETER READINGS (°F)					
		0°	5°	10°	15°	20°	
DRY BULB TEMPERATURE (°F)	85°	100	78	63	47	33	RELATIVE HUMIDITY (%)
	50°	100	68	38	15	1	

▲ **Examples from hygrometric tables.** A big difference in thermometer readings shows that the air is dry and relative humidity is low.

How clouds form

Clouds are made of millions of tiny, very light drops of water or particles of ice. They form when air is cooled below its dew point, or lower, and condensation happens. Water vapor always condenses out onto particles of smoke, dust and salt, floating in the air. Condensation doesn't happen in very clean, pure air.

The most usual way for clouds to form in cooling air begins when a warm patch of the earth's surface heats the air touching it. This creates a large bubble of warm air resting on the ground. The bubble rises through the denser, colder air above like a hot air balloon. As it rises, it expands and cools. A cloud forms when the rising bubble cools below its dew point. The cloud stops growing upwards when the bubble is too cold and heavy to rise any higher.

Warm air rising

Bubble of warm air expands and cools

Cloud forms when dew point is reached

Other clouds form in spread-out layers, rather than singly. This happens when rising bubbles of air, already cooled below their dew point, come up against a "ceiling" or "lid" of warmer air above.

This "lid" is a temperature inversion. In the troposphere, temperature usually falls with height, like pressure, but the temperature in an inversion rises or stays the same with height. Because the rising bubbles aren't buoyant enough to rise up through the inversion, they spread out underneath it, making sheets or layers of cloud.

Temperature inversions can happen very close to ground level. For example, on a clear, cloudless night, the air in contact with the ground cools rapidly below its dew point, so it's much cooler than the air above. Fog or mist (very low cloud) forms below the inversion and is trapped. In smoky cities, inversions often lead to smog (smoke-filled fog).

▲ **Smoke trapped below an inversion**

Cloud classification

Clouds are classified according to their height in the sky.

High-level clouds, averaging 20,000 feet up, are known as cirro-form clouds. They are wispy, delicate white clouds made of ice crystals.

Medium-level clouds, between six and twenty thousand feet, are known as alto-form clouds. They are thick white sheets of cloud made of water drops and ice crystals.

Low-level clouds, between the earth's surface and 6000 feet, are known as strato-form clouds. They are featureless gray layers of cloud made of water drops.

There is another group of clouds classified as low-level clouds and made of water drops. They are called cumulo-form clouds. They often push up through the higher levels and contain ice crystals as well. These clouds have flat bases and billowing white tops shaped like cauliflower heads.

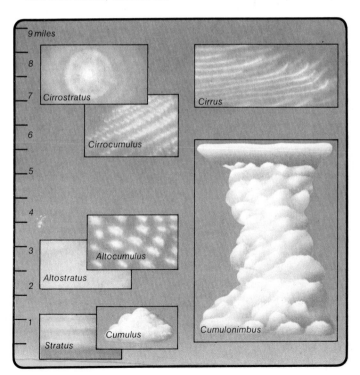

9 miles
8
7 Cirrostratus
Cirrus
6 Cirrocumulus
5
4
3 Altocumulus
Altostratus
2
1 Cumulus
Stratus
Cumulonimbus

High-level clouds

◄ Cirrus
Wispy streaks of high-level clouds made of ice crystals. They look like strands of hair, blown by the wind. This kind of cirrus is known as "mares' tails".

Cirrus ►
When there is very little wind at high levels in the sky, cirrus has a rather irregular, tangled appearance.

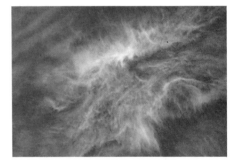

◄ Cirrocumulus
This cloud formation is often called a "mackerel sky". High clouds rippling across the sky, like the patterns wind and sand make on a beach.

Cirrostratus ▶

A thin veil of pale ice crystal cloud. In this picture, it only partly covers the sky. In the foreground there are puffs of fair weather cumulus clouds.

◀ Cirrostratus

Bands of cirrostratus in a pink sky. Although it is a fine evening, rain will arrive in the next day or two.
Cirrostratus, like cirrus, is an early warning sign of an approaching depression (see page 36).

Halo ▶

Rays of light bend when they fall on the ice crystals which make up cirrostratus. This creates a ring, known as a halo, around the sun or the moon.

15

Medium-level clouds

Altostratus ▶
This is a layer cloud like cirrostratus, but it is thicker, and lower in the sky. The sky looks milky, and the sun can just be seen.

◀ Nimbostratus
This is a thick rain cloud. ("Nimbus" is a Latin word, meaning rain.) Although it is classed as a medium-level cloud, it often extends into high and low levels in the sky.

Altocumulus ▶
A thicker, lower version of cirrocumulus. It looks like a layer of cotton balls. Altocumulus forms when bubbles of warm air rise and cool below their dew point.

◄ Altocumulus castellanus

Altocumulus clouds billowing upwards in rows. They look like turretted castle walls. They can be a sign of a summer thunderstorm.

Altocumulus lenticularis ►

Air rising to clear mountains sometimes keeps blowing up and down, in waves, on the other side. These "lee-wave clouds" form at the crest of the waves. They are quite rare, and look like cigars, lenses or flying saucers.

◄ Altocumulus and altostratus

A yellowish sunset sky with altocumulus merging into thick sheets of altostratus below. This sort of sky is an indication of unsettled weather.

Low-level clouds

◀ Stratus

Thick sheets of low-level cloud made of water drops. If it rests on the ground or the sea, it's fog. Stratus cloud usually brings drizzle (light snow in the winter).

◀ Stratus and Cumulus

The stratus overhead is in the warm sector of a depression. The bank of cumulus clouds in the distance, behind the line where the stratus ends, marks the approaching cold front. Stormy or showery weather ahead.

◀ Fracto-stratus

This name is given to stratus broken up into patches. These ragged gray clouds are evaporating as the warm front of a depression moves away and the rain stops.

◄ Fracto-stratus

Stratus cloud broken up by the wind on a summer day. It looks white in the sunshine, against the blue sky.

◄ Stratocumulus

Long, rolling bands of stratocumulus in a late afternoon sky, gradually drying out in the sunshine after a rainy day. Drier weather is on the way.

◄ Stratocumulus

A low layer of stratocumulus cloud trapped below an inversion, seen from an airplane. A patchwork of lumpy clouds in close rows.

Cumulo-form clouds

◄ Fair weather cumulus
Small puffs of cloud made by bubbles of warm air rising over the sea and cooling below their dew point. They evaporate away within minutes.

◄ Fair weather cumulus
Larger cumulus clouds, also formed by rising bubbles of warm air. Their flat bases mark the height where the air reaches its dew point and condensation begins.

◄ Cumulus
Cumulus clouds formed orographically – by air cooling when it is forced to rise over high ground (in this case, a range of mountains).

Cumulus and hill fog ▶

Some of these clouds (formed orographically) are stranded on the ground as hill fog. The air trying to get over the mountains has become too cold and heavy to rise any higher.

Cumulus ▶

Very large cumulus, just turning into cumulonimbus, arriving on the cold front of a depression. There will soon be heavy showers or storms.

Cumulonimbus ▶

A huge thundercloud. Its towering top is made of ice crystals. A cumulonimbus may reach the height of the tropopause. It brings stormy showers of rain, snow or hail.

◄ Cumulonimbus

When a cumulonimbus cloud can't rise any higher, its top spreads out into the shape of an anvil, blown in the direction of the winds at its level. This one has come up against an inversion of temperature.

Cloud street ►

Cumulus clouds occasionally spread out and join up parallel to the direction of the wind. This formation is known as a "street" or a "line".

◄ Mamma

Large blobs of cloud hanging down from the base of a cumulonimbus cloud, like a giant udder. Mamma are a sign of strong winds and heavy rain.

◀Look out for and photograph spectacular cloud effects like this one. The best times to take photographs are sunrise and sunset.

Notice how in this picture the sky near the setting sun (lit by rays of direct sunlight) is a rich orange color, while the sky at the top of the picture (lit by rays of indirect sunlight) is almost violet.

The weather maps made at weather stations use symbols to show the type and amount of cloud seen in the sky at a certain time. In order to judge cloud amount, the sky is divided into oktas (eighths).

Cloud Cover

Clear sky	1 okta	2 oktas
3 oktas	4 oktas	5 oktas
6 oktas	7 oktas	Overcast

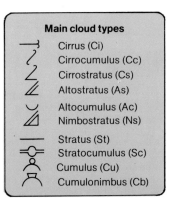

Main cloud types

Cirrus (Ci)
Cirrocumulus (Cc)
Cirrostratus (Cs)
Altostratus (As)
Altocumulus (Ac)
Nimbostratus (Ns)
Stratus (St)
Stratocumulus (Sc)
Cumulus (Cu)
Cumulonimbus (Cb)

Precipitation

Precipitation – water falling from the sky in solid or liquid form. For example, rain, snow, sleet and hail.

The millions of water drops, ice particles and ice crystals that make up one cloud are extremely small (the smallest raindrop is a hundred times larger than most cloud drops). Before they can fall out of the cloud as precipitation they must grow much larger and heavier. They do this either by coalescing (see below) or condensing (or by a mixture of both).

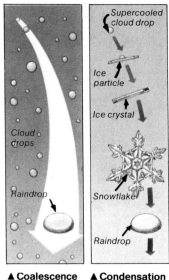

▲ **Coalescence**
Large cloud drop absorbs smaller ones as it falls.

▲ **Condensation**
Ice particles slowly build up and turn into raindrops.

Condensation

Condensation generally happens in clouds containing both water drops and ice particles. It causes long periods of rain, snow or drizzle. The water drops in the cloud aren't frozen, although the temperature of the cloud may be well below freezing. They are said to be supercooled. Some of these supercooled cloud drops evaporate; the water vapor tends to condense and freeze onto the ice particles. The ice particles get bigger; they become ice crystals, which join together and make snowflakes. The snowflakes are large and heavy enough to fall out of the cloud. If they drop down through warmer air, they melt and fall as rain.

Coalescence

Short, sharp showers generally happen because of coalescence of water drops in rain clouds. The larger drops inside the cloud are blown upwards by air currents. As they rise they coalesce – they bump into and absorb smaller drops, and grow bigger and bigger. By the time they reach the top of the cloud, they are so large and heavy that they fall down again, absorb more cloud drops, and fall right out at the bottom of the cloud, as raindrops. Some of the smaller raindrops evaporate away as they fall through warmer air. The raindrops we see are the largest ones produced by clouds.

Hail

Hail falls from cumulonimbus clouds, huge towering clouds made of water drops and ice particles. A hailstone starts out as an ice particle.

Ice particles build up into ice crystals by condensation. The ice crystals are blown up and down inside the cloud by very strong air currents, and as they are thrown around, they absorb more and more cloud drops.

The cloud drops freeze onto the ice crystals in layers, like the skins of an onion. When they freeze near the warmer, lower part of the cloud, they freeze fairly slowly, and spread out as a layer of clear ice. When they freeze near the higher, colder part of the cloud, they freeze instantly, making a layer of frosty ice.

By counting the layers of ice in a hailstone, we can tell how many times it was blown up and down inside the cloud, just as we can tell how old a tree is by counting the rings in its trunk.

The more violent the air currents are, the taller the cloud will grow, and the bigger the hailstones are likely to be. Most hailstones are less than two inches in diameter, but they grow much larger on occasions.

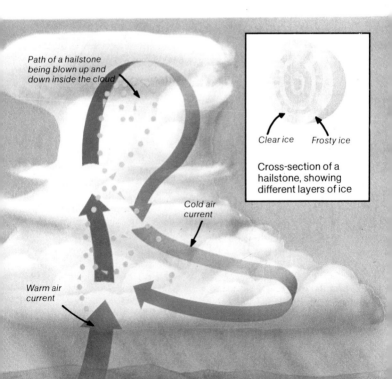

Path of a hailstone being blown up and down inside the cloud

Clear ice   Frosty ice

Cross-section of a hailstone, showing different layers of ice

Cold air current

Warm air current

Thunder and lightning

Thunderstorms, sometimes called electric storms, are created by cumulonimbus clouds. Violent air currents blowing up and down inside the cloud tear the largest cloud drops apart and force ice crystals, supercooled drops and hailstones to crash into each other. All this turbulence creates friction, which charges the broken bits and pieces with static electricity. Light, positively charged (+) drops pile up at the top of the cloud, and heavy, negatively charged (–) drops pile up at the bottom. The ground below the cloud is also charged with positive electricity.

Sooner or later, the negative charge in the bottom of the cloud discharges itself into the ground in an electrical spark – a flash of lightning. This first flash is called the leader stroke. The positive charge in the ground then runs up to the cloud along the narrow path forged in the air by the leader stroke. This makes a second flash, called the return stroke. It is much brighter than the leader stroke, and contains millions of volts of electricity.

Air is a poor conductor of electricity, but the resistance of the narrow path of air is destroyed by the enormous power in the return stroke. The air becomes extremely hot and expands at supersonic speed. This makes the deafening crash we call thunder.

Lightning travels at a speed of 186,000 miles per second, while

▲ Electrical charges build up in the cloud, positive (+) at the top, negative (–) at the bottom.

thunder travels at only 1100 feet per second. This is why you hear thunder some time after you see lightning, even though they happen at exactly the same time.

If you hear thunder five seconds after you saw a flash of lightning the thunderstorm is about one mile away.

Leader and return strokes happen separately, but so quickly that we see them as a single stroke. Sheet lightning is just lightning sparking between opposite charges inside clouds; we see a glow reflected by the flash, not the strokes themselves.

Conductor – metal is a good conductor of electricity; it allows electricity to flow through it. Wood and rubber are poor conductors; they resist electricity.

▲ Leader stroke discharges the negative charge in the cloud into the positively charged ground.

▲ Return stroke flashes up from the ground, heating the air. The air expands with a bang – thunder.

▲ Strokes of lightning flashing between a cloud and the ground as a storm travels along, moving from left to right. The glow to the right is sheet lightning.

Lightning always takes the quickest path it can find from a cloud down to the ground. If often runs down high objects standing alone, like church steeples and flagpoles. Most tall buildings are protected by lightning conductors, metal strips that carry the electricity safely into the ground if the building is struck by lightning.

If you are caught outside during a thunderstorm, keep away from trees, television antennas and metal fences. Don't lie down or stand upright – crouch. You are safe inside buildings if you keep away from the walls. You are also safe inside a car.

Wind

Winds are caused by differences in temperature and pressure. There is high pressure on the earth's surface where cold, heavy air is sinking, and low pressure where warm, light air is rising. The low latitudes (areas between the Equator and 30° north and south) receive a lot of the sun's energy and are very hot, while the high latitudes (areas between the North or South Poles and 60° north or south) receive very little of the sun's energy and are very cold. Warm air rising near the Equator blows towards the Poles and is replaced by cool air blowing in underneath it from higher latitudes.

If the earth stood still, winds would keep to this basic north-south pattern. But the earth rotates, spinning on its axis, like a top. The Equator moves fastest, the Poles hardly move at all. This changes the general movement of air over the earth, giving us mainly westerly winds (from the west) in the middle latitudes (30° to 60° north and south) and mainly easterly winds (from the east) in the other latitudes.

Imagine you're in a spacecraft high above the earth, and you see a rocket fired from the North Pole. The rocket appears to be flying south in a straight line, and it lands a hundred miles south of the Pole. However, anyone on earth would tell you that the rocket's flight path curved to the right; they would insist that it landed west of the point where it would have landed, had it really been traveling in a straight line. This is because the earth rotates from west to east. While the rocket was in the air, the earth moved several degrees to the east.

In the same way, winds do not blow directly northward and southward between the Poles and the Equator. Winds in the northern hemisphere bend to their right, winds in the southern hemisphere, to their left.

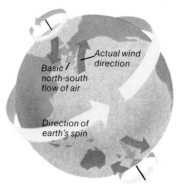

Basic north-south flow of air

Actual wind direction

Direction of earth's spin

▲ The earth rotates from west to east. This changes the basic north-south flow of air over the earth. Winds in the northern hemisphere swerve to their right, winds in the southern hemisphere, to their left, giving us mainly westerlies and easterlies.

> **Latitude** – distance north or south of the Equator, measured in degrees (The latitude of the Equator is 0°).

This is how the westerly and easterly winds come about: air warmed at the Equator rises and blows as wind towards the Poles. At about 30° north and south, air piles up and makes belts of high pressure. Some of this air cools, sinks and blows as wind to the Equator. Because of the earth's rotation, these winds swerve off course, becoming northeasterly winds in the northern hemisphere and southeasterly winds in the southern hemisphere. These winds are known as trade winds. Other winds blow away from the high-pressure belts and carry on towards the Poles. They swerve too, and turn into westerly winds. At about 60° north and south, there are low-pressure belts where the weather is generally unsettled.

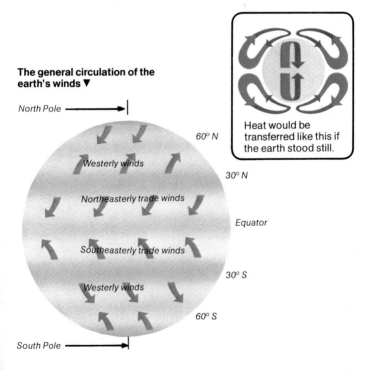

The general circulation of the earth's winds ▼

North Pole ───────▶|

60° N

Westerly winds

30° N

Northeasterly trade winds

Equator

Southeasterly trade winds

30° S

Westerly winds

60° S

South Pole ───────▶|

Heat would be transferred like this if the earth stood still.

Wind and pressure

There is high pressure wherever air sinks and low pressure wherever air rises. Winds blow from high- to low-pressure areas.

Centers of high pressure are called anticyclones; centers of low pressure are called cyclones. On weather maps, they are marked by isobars, lines joining places of the same pressure. If the isobars are close together, it means there is a steep pressure gradient – there is a big difference in pressure between places close to each other. The steeper the pressure gradient, the faster the winds will be.

Winds blow almost parallel to isobars, instead of straight across them, because the rotation of the earth. They spiral away from anti-cyclones, moving clockwise in the northern hemisphere and count-erclockwise in the southern hemis-phere. They spiral in toward depressions, moving counter-clockwise in the northern hemis-phere and clockwise in the southern hemisphere. If you stand with your back to the wind, the lower pressure is always on your left in the northern hemisphere, and on your right in the southern hemisphere.

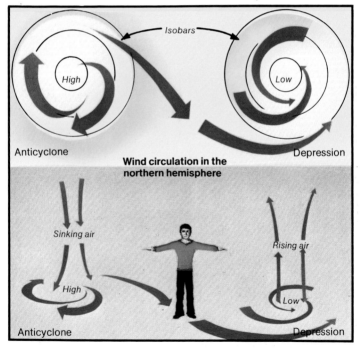

Wind circulation in the northern hemisphere

Wind speed

Wind speed can be judged in several ways. You can tell if the wind is blowing hard or not simply by watching trees, clothes hanging on a line, or anything else outside. Anemometers measure wind speed accurately. There are many different kinds; the cup anemometer, for example, consists of three or four cups on the ends of horizontal arms, attached to a central, vertical shaft. The wind catches the cups and blows them around, making the central shaft spin. The number of turns the shaft makes in one minute is recorded on a dial or counter, and the figure recorded is converted into knots, or miles or kilometers per hour.

You often see a wind vane attached near an anemometer. Wind vanes are used to find out wind direction. They have a horizontal arm with an arrow at one end and a fin at the other. The wind blows the fin around and the arrow points to the direction the wind is coming from.

▲ Cup anemometer and wind vane

Wind speed symbols

⊙	Calm	
	1–2	knots
	3–7	knots
	8–12	knots
	13–17	knots
	18–22	knots
	23–27	knots
	28–32	knots
	33–37	knots
	38–42	knots
	43–47	knots
▲	48–52	knots

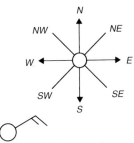

▲ This symbol on a weather map would indicate a northeasterly wind (from the northeast) blowing at a speed of about 15 knots.

Local winds

There are many small scale, local winds that influence the weather in different parts of the world. The simplest kind of local wind is the land-sea breeze, which happens on coasts. During the day, the land heats up faster than the sea; air rising over the land is replaced by a cool, onshore sea breeze. At night, the land cools faster than the sea, so a land breeze blows offshore, to the sea.

The monsoon winds of India and Asia are large scale, seasonal versions of the land-sea breeze. India, for example, gets steadily hotter during the spring and early summer. In June, monsoon winds begin to blow onshore, full of moisture evaporated from the Indian Ocean and the Bay of Bengal. These winds are forced to rise when they blow over high ground, and this makes them cool down. Clouds form, and torrential rains begin to fall.

During the winter months, the land is cooler than the sea. Dry winds blow offshore. These dry monsoon winds can make the land barren and arid; if the summer monsoon winds are late, India's crops die from lack of water and many people are likely to starve.

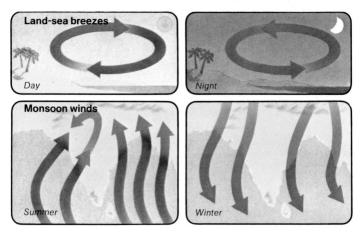

Land-sea breezes — Day / Night

Monsoon winds — Summer / Winter

Katabatic winds are mountain winds found in places like Norway. They blow on clear nights. Air in contact with the cold, snowy mountain slopes cools very quickly at dusk; it sinks down and collects in a cold pool beneath the warmer air in the valleys below. Katabatic winds tend to cause frosts, which damage crops growing in the valleys.

The Chinook wind that blows in the Rocky Mountains of North America is a föhn wind. It is a wind that loses its moisture blowing over the Rockies from the West, and then blows dry and warm down the other side, melting winter snows on the plains of the eastern slopes.

Jet streams

The tropopause isn't exactly the same height in all parts of the world. Warm air rising above the Equator pushes the tropopause up to a height of 10 miles, while cold air sinking over the Poles allows the tropopause to drop down to about 5½ miles.

Sudden, wide differences in the temperature of the atmosphere create sharp pressure differences. Where these differences are particularly sharp, they split the tropopause. It isn't so much a smooth, uniform layer of air, as a series of gigantic, overlapping plates of air. Extremely fast winds blow along the breaks in the tropopause. These winds are known as jet streams.

Jet streams are winds shaped like squashed tubes, thousands of miles long, and hundreds of miles wide. Wind speed at the central core of the "tubes" reaches 100 knots or more (surface winds rarely exceed 30 knots because mountains, buildings and other obstacles slow them down). Jet streams blow mainly from west to east.

The sharpest differences in the temperatures of the polar and tropical regions happen in the winter months, when the sun is lowest in the sky. This is when jet streams are most marked.

There is an extremely fast jet stream over the North Atlantic. Planes flying from New York to London along this jet stream can arrive in only six hours. The return journey will take at least an hour longer, even if they avoid flying into the jet stream.

▼ Part of the northern hemisphere with a section of the troposphere stripped away to show a jet stream.

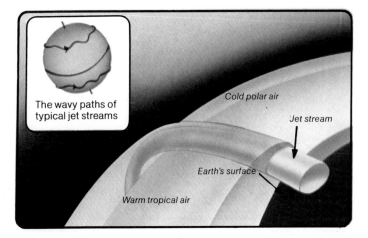

The wavy paths of typical jet streams

Cold polar air

Jet stream

Earth's surface

Warm tropical air

Air masses

Air masses are huge masses of air with the same temperature and humidity. They are caused when an area of air hundreds of miles wide rests on a sea or a land mass that has a fairly even temperature and humidity. The air takes on the characteristics of the surface below. There are two extreme kinds of air masses – tropical ones, which are warm, and polar ones, which are cold.

Air moves over the earth's surface, trying to even out the distribution of heat. As air masses leave the place where they formed, they become modified, warming up or cooling down, becoming drier or moister, according to the different surfaces they travel over. Meanwhile, fresh supplies of polar and tropical air are being produced at the Poles and in the Tropics.

Very different air masses don't mix together when they meet. There is a polar front in each hemisphere, a boundary between modified polar and tropical air masses. These boundaries are belts of unsettled weather.

On weather maps, air masses are labeled to show where they came from. Air masses from the Poles are labeled P, air masses from the Tropics, T. If they formed over land, they are labeled c (for continental), if they formed over sea or ocean, m (for maritime). So an air mass labeled cP came from a polar land mass, like Alaska, for example, while an air mass labeled mT came from a tropical sea, like the Carribean.

mP   cP   mT   cT   Polar front

▲ The average paths of air masses from the Poles and the Tropics

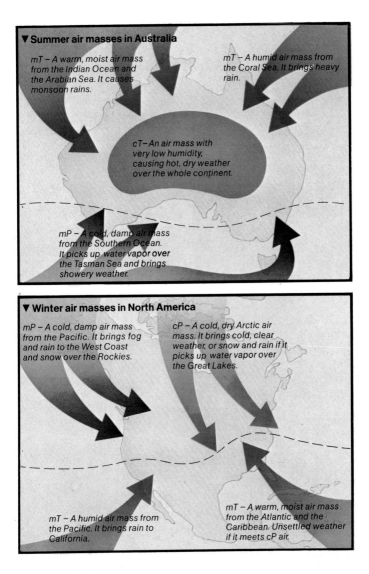

▼ **Summer air masses in Australia**

mT – A warm, moist air mass from the Indian Ocean and the Arabian Sea. It causes monsoon rains.

mT – A humid air mass from the Coral Sea. It brings heavy rain.

cT – An air mass with very low humidity, causing hot, dry weather over the whole continent.

mP – A cold, damp air mass from the Southern Ocean. It picks up water vapor over the Tasman Sea and brings showery weather.

▼ **Winter air masses in North America**

mP – A cold, damp air mass from the Pacific. It brings fog and rain to the West Coast and snow over the Rockies.

cP – A cold, dry Arctic air mass. It brings cold, clear weather, or snow and rain if it picks up water vapor over the Great Lakes.

mT – A humid air mass from the Pacific. It brings rain to California.

mT – A warm, moist air mass from the Atlantic and the Caribbean. Unsettled weather if it meets cP air.

Depressions

The struggles between polar air masses moving towards the Equator and tropical air masses moving towards the Poles create depressions along the polar fronts. Depressions bring rainy or stormy unsettled weather.

The pictures below show how a depression forms along the polar front in the northern hemisphere (this polar front is particularly marked during the winter). First of all, some of the warm, moist tropical air in the south bulges into the colder, drier polar air on the north side of the polar front. The warm air rises over the cold air, jutting into it like a tongue.

Pressure drops on the earth's surface below the rising warm air. Pressure is lowest just below the northernmost tip of the tongue of warm air; this spot becomes the center of the depression. Cold polar air rushes in from the north to replace the rising warm air, and

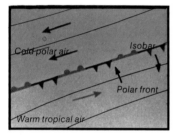

1. Polar front (northern hemisphere). Cold polar air in the north, warm tropical air in the south.

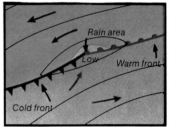

2. Ten hours later. The warm air juts into the cold air and makes a dent in the polar front.

▼ **Block diagram of a fully developed depression**

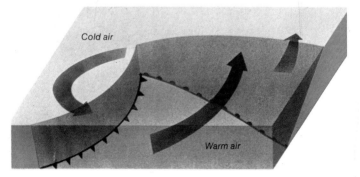

spirals in toward the center of the depression. A circulation of air, cold chasing warm, begins.

The warm air mass advances northward by rising up over the cold air in a gradual slope. The cold air mass advances southward by undercutting the warm air like a steep wedge, lifting it up from behind. The edge of the advancing warm air is called a warm front, the edge of the advancing cold air is a cold front. Clouds form along each front, where the cold and warm air meet. Each front is hundreds of miles long.

The depression will probably move more or less eastward blown along by the strongest winds in the upper levels of the sky (often jet streams). Depressions die down once the faster moving cold front catches up with the warm front; the fronts merge in a single rainy front, known as an occluded front or occlusion.

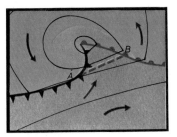

3. Twenty hours later. A fully developed depression, with a cold front chasing a warm front.

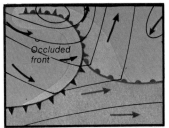

4. Thirty hours later. The cold front catches up with the warm front and they merge together.

▼ **Cross-section from A to B in the third diagram (above)**

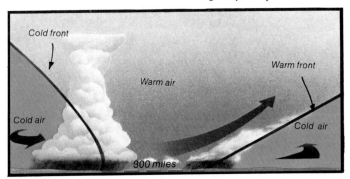

Warm and cold fronts

The first sign of an approaching depression is long streaks of cirrus in the sky, soon followed by cirrostratus. Then pressure begins to fall and the wind backs (see above) and becomes stronger. (All wind direction changes are opposite in the southern hemisphere, where the wind would veer at this point.)

As the warm front arrives, the clouds thicken into altostratus and nimbostratus. Heavy rain or snow starts to fall.

The rain or snow continues until the warm front has passed. Then pressure stops falling, the wind might veer, and the temperature rises. Visibility is still poor. Thinner layers of stratus cloud replace the nimbostratus, and light snow or drizzle falls.

Then the warm sector – the area between the two fronts – arrives. It brings calmer, milder weather. Temperature, wind and pressure

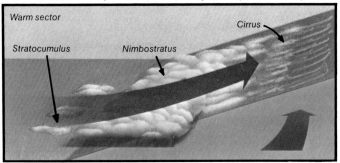

▲ The gradual slope of a warm front; warm tropical air rising over the cold polar air ahead.

▲ The first sign of a warm front; cirrus increasing to cirrostratus.

▲ A warm front moving away; altostratus above fracto-stratus.

stay fairly steady. If the sunshine is strong enough, the clouds will dry out and become stratocumulus; otherwise, there will probably be fog or drizzle for a while.

As the more violent cold front approaches, the wind backs and blows harder, in gusts. Pressure falls, but the temperature stays steady. Then a solid bank of cumulus, altostratus and cumulonimbus advances, bringing heavy showers of rain or snow. There may even be thunderstorms or hail showers when the cold front is directly overhead.

Once the cold front has moved away, the temperature drops, but pressure rises and visibility improves dramatically. The sky is clear and blue, usually dotted with a few fair weather cumulus clouds. There may still be one or two showers if the clouds thicken and merge together, however.

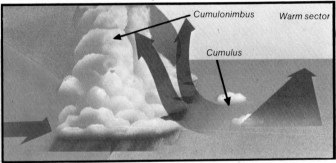

▲ The steep wedge of a cold front; cold polar air undercutting the warm tropical air ahead.

▲ Towering cumulo-form clouds on an advancing cold front.

▲ A cold front moving away; blue sky appearing.

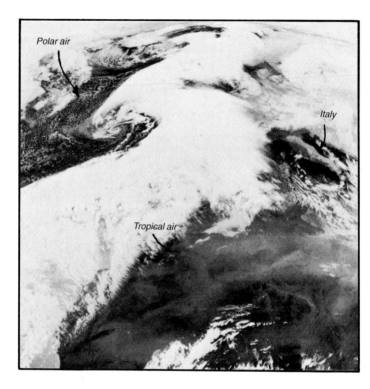

Polar air

Italy

Tropical air

▲ This photograph was taken by a satellite camera. It shows a depression over western Europe, moving more or less eastward.

There is a marked difference between the humid tropical air occupying the lower part of the photograph and the crisp polar air above. The tropical air looks grayish, blurred with strato-form clouds, while the polar air looks black, speckled with cumulo-form shower clouds.

The swirling white mass in the center of the photograph is cloud in the warm sector of the depression, between the warm and cold fronts.

Notice the curling shape at the center of the depression, where the polar air is spiraling in below the rising warm air; it looks rather like water going down a plughole. They are anticyclones over northern Africa and over Italy, that can be clearly seen.

Occluded fronts

When the cold front of a depression catches up with the warm front, they merge together in a single, occluded front. Occlusions are belts of rain or snow, a combination of warm and cold front weather conditions.

The warm sector between the two fronts is the tongue of warm tropical air that jutted into the cold polar air mass and started the depression in the first place. When the fronts occlude, they squeeze the warm sector between them, like a giant finger and thumb pinching together. The warm sector air is separated from the rest of the tropical air mass and lifted right up, off the surface of the earth. None of the warm sector air touches the surface any longer; it is just a pool of warm air resting on top of the cold polar air. The only sign of it below is a shallow low-pressure area.

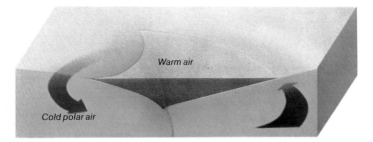

▲ Block diagram of an occlusion. The warm and cold fronts have closed up, pinching the warm sector between them and lifting it up.

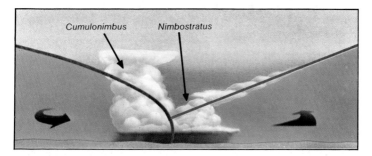

▲ Cross-section of an occlusion. The clouds on the warm and cold fronts have joined up. A pool of warm air, all that remains of the warm sector, rests on top of the cold polar air mass.

Anticyclonic weather

▲ In the summer, anticyclones can bring hot, dry, sunny weather.

▲ Winter anticyclones either bring fogs or bitter cold and frosts.

An anticyclone is a huge mass of sinking air. As it sinks, it warms up and dries out the clouds in the sky. When it comes up against a cooler air mass resting on the surface of the earth, it can't sink any lower, so an inversion is created.

In the summer, when the ground and the air close to it are warm and fairly dry, anticyclones can lead to hot, sunny days and blue skies – even heatwaves. Any dew or mist forming below the inversion during the night, when the ground radiates its heat away quickly, soon evaporates in the hot sunshine the next morning.

In the winter, anticyclones can still lead to cloudless blue skies and sunny weather, but because there aren't any clouds in the sky to trap the earth's radiation, temperatures are very low. Also, the fog and frost which tend to form at night below the inversion take a long time to disappear in the weak winter sunshine.

Anticyclones move slowly and don't bring much wind or rain, so anticyclonic weather is usually drier and more settled than the weather that depressions tend to bring. However, anticyclones cause severe frosts and fogs and bitter cold in winter as well as sunny skies.

Clouds form when air rises and expands because air cools when it expands. For example, when the compressed air in an aerosol can is released, it expands instantly; that's why the spray is cold. But clouds don't form in a sinking air mass because the air is compressed as it sinks; air warms up and dries out when it is compressed. For example, your bicycle pump heats up when you use it because it is compressing air, forcing it into the tire along a very narrow tube.

Troughs, ridges and cols

Here are some more pressure features you may see on weather maps.
In name and appearance, they are like relief features on contour maps.

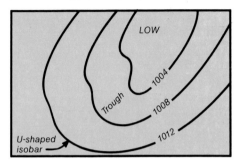

◄ Trough

A trough of low pressure looks like a valley on a contour map. It is marked by open, U-shaped isobars, with lower pressure on the inside of the "U's". Troughs are extensions of depressions, and bring cloudy, showery weather as a rule.

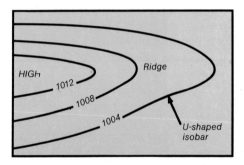

◄ Ridge

A ridge of high pressure looks like a ridge or spur on a contour map. It is marked by open, U-shaped isobars, with higher pressure on the inside of the "U's". Ridges are extensions of anticyclones, and bring the same kind of weather as anticyclones.

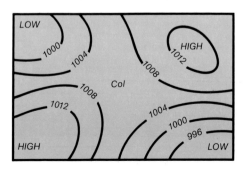

◄ Col

A col looks like a col or saddle on a contour map. It is the neutral area between alternating depressions and anticyclones (two of each). Cols bring no particular kind of weather apart from light, variable winds. They never last very long.

Tropical storms

In the tropical seas near the Equator, depressions can turn into violent tropical storms with hurricane force winds and torrential rains. These storms form along the boundary where the trade winds of either hemisphere, blowing in opposite directions, meet. They have different names in the various seas where they happen. They are known as cyclones in the Indian Ocean and the Bay of Bengal, typhoons in the China Seas, hurricanes in the Caribbean and Willy-willies off the coasts of Australia.

Tropical storms only develop in very humid air with a temperature over 79°F, so they happen mostly in the summer and early autumn, when the seas and the air above are at their warmest.

First of all, the warm sea heats the air above. A current of very warm, moist air rises quickly above the sea, creating a center of very low pressure on the surface below. Trade winds rush in towards this low-pressure center and whirl upwards. As they rise, they cool, and the huge amounts of water vapor they contain condense out and form towering cumulus and cumulonimbus clouds. At the center of the massive, spiraling storm, with its huge clouds and driving rain, is a calm core, the "eye" of the storm, which is about 25 miles wide.

Some of the latent heat released when the storm clouds form is thrown into the eye. This makes it about five degrees hotter than the rest of the storm and keeps it dry and free of clouds. The eye is also calm and still, even though winds roaring the belts of cloud around it reach speeds of between 65 and 150 knots.

On weather maps, a tropical storm is drawn by very tight, closed, almost circular isobars, with pressure in the eye as low as 960 mb. Surprisingly, although the air in the eye is warmer than the rest of the storm, it is slowly sinking down to the surface of the sea.

▲ Infrared satellite picture (processed into color) taken on August 18, 1969. It shows the whirling storm clouds of Hurricane Camille (blue) crossing the warm waters of the Gulf of Mexico (mauve) towards the coastlands of the Misssissppi (red). The large blue patches north and south of the circular storm are clouds associated with it.

The power to drive the storm comes from the latent heat which is released when moisture in the trade winds condenses and forms clouds. But once the storm leaves the warm air above the tropical seas, it loses its power source and dies down altogether. This usually happens after a week or so, when the storm travels across cooler waters, or across a land mass.

While tropical storms last, they do tremendous amounts of damage, wrecking ships and buildings, flooding rivers with their heavy rains, and whipping up tidal waves. Weather radar, reconnaissance aircraft and satellites keep careful watch for the first sign of a depression developing into a tropical storm, so that the areas likely to be affected can be warned.

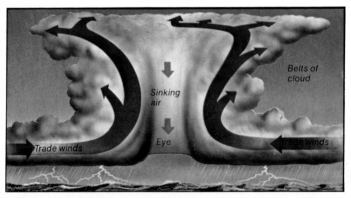

▲ Section of a tropical storm, showing trade winds being swept in at the base of the eye, rising up, and being thrown out at the top.

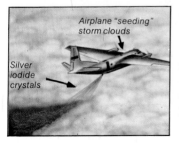

One way to stop a depression turning into a full-blown tropical storm is to "seed" the clouds with silver iodide crystals. These are artificial condensation nuclei. Water drops in the clouds collect on them, coalesce and rain down, damping down the strong up-currents of warm air which build the clouds up to dangerous heights.

Tornadoes

Tornadoes are violent, twisting whirlwinds – funnel-shaped clouds extending down from the base of cumulonimbus clouds. Although they are much smaller than tropical storms (about 300 feet across) they cause tremendous damage. Exactly why they happen isn't certain but, like tropical storms, they form in humid air where winds blow into each other from opposite directions. They happen over land, not water, and are usually accompanied by heavy rain, thunder and lightning.

There is an extremely strong upward current of air in a tornado. It sucks up or destroys everything in its path, including people, animals, trees and vehicles. (A tornado once lifted a railroad car, with the passengers inside it, over 65 feet into the air before dropping it onto the ground). The pressure gradient near the center is so steep that buildings explode instantly when a tornado moves over them.

Even if the right instruments were in the path of a tornado at the right time, they would not survive the violence of the impact, so it is difficult to get precise wind and pressure readings. However, it is likely that pressure in the center of a tornado is as low as 500 mb, and that winds hurtling upwards inside it and whirling around it reach speeds of up to 200 knots. Tornadoes can travel hundreds of miles before they die down.

Tornadoes form in the summer, mainly in North America, and less often in Australia, South America, southern Africa and Europe.

▲ Wreckage flying about in the air as a huge tornado whirls through a town

◄Waterspout

Like tornadoes, waterspouts are whirlwinds extending down from cumulonimbus clouds. They form over seas and lakes, mainly in the Tropics, and look like columns of water. They churn up the water below and suck it up in a spiral. Waterspouts have often been mistaken for long-necked sea monsters. They range from a few yards to a few hundred yards high, and they last about half an hour.

◄Funnel cloud

Funnel clouds are miniature versions of tornadoes and waterspouts, and extend down from the base of cumulonimbus clouds. They can form in any part of the world.

Dust devil ►

Dust devils grow upward from the ground, not down from clouds. They happen in hot deserts, like the Namib Desert in South Africa. Little spirals of warm air rise off the baked earth, sweeping up dust, so they look like columns of dust. They are about 100 feet high, and last only a few minutes.

Weather forecasts

If you are planning an outdoor activity, like sailing, riding, having a picnic, or even just a long walk, it is a good idea to find out what kind of weather conditions to expect, so you can set off properly prepared.

There are several ways of finding out how the weather is likely to change. National weather reports and forecasts are broadcast on the television and the radio and printed in newspapers. Regional forecasts are prepared by weather stations. You can telephone your local weather service station and hear a recorded broadcast.

In addition to all their usual broadcasts, radio stations also give special warnings of dangerous weather conditions, like tornadoes, hurricanes, or blizzards.

The best way for you to get up-to-date information about the weather in your area is to telephone your local weather station and ask for any particular details you need.

Weather forecasters explain in simpler terms the information they get from computer forecast maps, satellite photographs and synoptic charts (see page 50). A weather forecast will tell you about the wind, precipitation, and the highest and lowest temperatures expected during the next 24 hours. It may also give some idea of what the weather is going to be like in the next few days as well. Forecasts covering longer periods, like a whole month, are bound to be much less reliable than those for 24, 36 or 48 hours ahead.

▲ Listen to the forecasts before you go sailing. Pay special attention to small craft warnings. Depressions tend to cause choppy seas, strong, changeable winds, a lot of low cloud and possibly fog as well.

▲ If you go hiking or rock climbing, watch out for mist and hill fog, which can fall suddenly in hilly country. The risk of fog is greatest in anticyclonic weather, and when relative humidity is high.

Television and newspaper forecasts

As well as using maps and satellite pictures, weather forecasts on television can show clouds, rain and snow on a radar screen.

Radar scanners radiate beams that cover an area within about 125 miles of the scanner. Large cloud drops and precipitation reflect the beams and send back echo signals just as larger objects like ships and airplanes do. The clouds and precipitation picked up by the scanner show up on a screen as bright patches. Radar is useful for tracking belts of rain and storms.

▲ The bright, curling streak on this radar screen is a tropical storm.

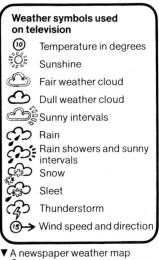

Weather symbols used on television

(10)	Temperature in degrees
☼	Sunshine
☁	Fair weather cloud
☁	Dull weather cloud
☼☁	Sunny intervals
☔	Rain
☔☼	Rain showers and sunny intervals
❄☁	Snow
☁	Sleet
⚡☁	Thunderstorm
(15)→	Wind speed and direction

Some newspapers print two kinds of weather maps: one reporting the actual state of the weather, and another forecasting weather changes.

It takes a long time to produce and distribute a newspaper, so the forecast maps are plotted many hours before you see them. This is why they are often inaccurate or out-of-date compared with forecasts on the radio and television, which can be updated with fresh information all the time.

▼ A newspaper weather map

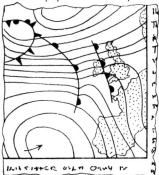

Synoptic charts

Every hour of the day and night, weather stations all over the world make observations of pressure, temperature, wind, cloud and humidity, and relay the information by teleprinter to a national weather office. Other observations come in from weather ships and buoys, airplanes, radio sondes, merchant ships, satellites and automatic weather recording stations in remote parts of the world.

At the national weather office, a weather map, called a synoptic chart, is drawn up. Each weather station is marked on it by a circle, and the information it sent in is marked around it in code numbers and symbols recognized all over the world. The weather service then studies the map and draws in the isobars and fronts. The synoptic chart is now a picture of the pressure patterns over a wide area at the time the observations were made.

The information on synoptic charts is fed into a computer several times a day. The computer analyzes it and prints out maps forecasting how pressure patterns – therefore weather conditions – are likely to change in the next few days.

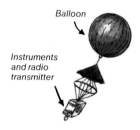

▲ A radio sonde is a gas-filled balloon carrying instruments that transmit observations of pressure, temperature and humidity to receivers on the earth's surface by radio. When it reaches a height of 18½ miles, the balloon bursts and the instruments float down by parachute.

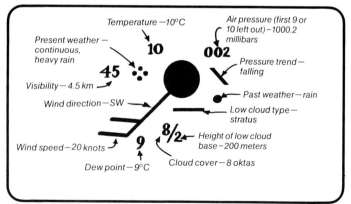

▲ Model of a station circle on a synoptic chart

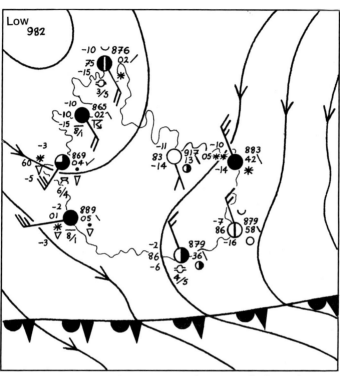

▲ This is a small section of a synoptic chart. At the time of observation, there were stormy showers in the northwest of Iceland, clear weather in the center, and strong northerlies and snow on the northeast coast. The center of low pressure in the northwest is moving towards the southeast, where pressure is falling.

Weather symbols			
Mist		Continuous heavy rain
Fog		Snow
Drizzle		Hail
Rain		Shower
Continuous moderate rain		Thunderstorm

Weather satellites

Weather satellites take pictures of the clouds over the earth. They help weather forecasters to predict how weather conditions are likely to change over a wide area. Some of these satellites are geostationary; this means that they hover above the earth in a fixed position. Others orbit the earth, moving from Pole to Pole.

Satellites are equipped with television cameras that scan the earth as it rotates below, then transmit signals to receivers on the earth's surface. These signals can then be changed into pictures.

Some satellite pictures are taken in the visible light wavelength. They are photographs of the sunlight reflected by the earth. The brightest areas in these pictures are clouds and snow, the darkest, oceans and seas. Other satellite pictures are taken in the infrared wavelength. They are pictures of the heat radiated by the earth. The brightest areas in these pictures are also clouds (because clouds are so cold), the darkest areas are the hottest - deserts, for example.

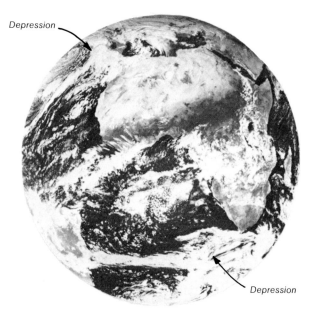

Depression

Depression

▲ This is a visible light photograph, taken by a geostationary satellite hovering at a height of 22,000 miles above the earth. Notice the depressions along the polar fronts, shown by white belts of cloud.

Satellite

Receiver

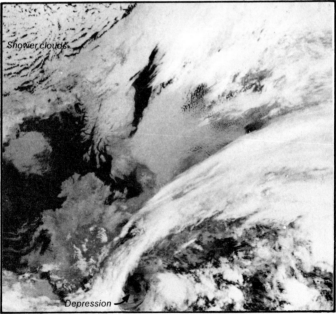

Shower clouds

Depression —

▲ This infrared satellite picture shows shower clouds over the sea north of Scotland, and swirling depression over southern England, where crisp polar air has met warmer, moister air.

▲ This visible light satellite photograph shows a broad band of cloud over western Europe, marking the northern hemisphere polar front.

▼ A visible light photograph showing a humid tropical air mass moving towards Britain. (The dotted white outlines are added by computer.)

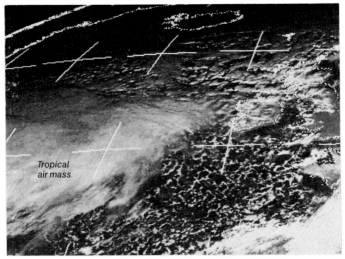

Making a weather station

By making your own weather observations, you will be able to recognize different pressure systems and see how they affect the weather in your area. This will help you to make weather forecasts of your own.

To set up a weather station at home or at school, you need a barometer, a rain gauge, a wind sock, a hygrometer, a thermometer and a maximum/minimum thermometer.

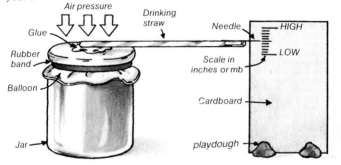

Barometer

Barometers are usually expensive, so if you don't already have one, you may like to make one. You will need:

A wide-mouthed jar
A rubber balloon
A drinking straw
All-purpose glue
A thick rubber band
Cardboard
A needle
Clear tape
A ruler
A pen
Scissors
Playdough

Cut off the neck of the balloon, and stretch the rest of it tightly over the mouth of the jar. Slip the rubber band around the neck of the jar to keep the balloon in space. Tape the needle to one end of the drinking straw to center of the balloon. Then mark off a scale in inches on the cardboard, and stand it up behind the pointer. Anchor it with lumps of playdough. Set up the barometer inside or outside (as long as it's not in the sun).

The pointer will move up and down the scale as air presses more or less on the balloon, and show you if pressure is rising or falling. To make a milibar scale, borrow a barometer. Then note on your scale, next to the pointer, the milibar figure registered by the borrowed barometer. Do this over several days to get as wide a range in pressure as possible.

Thermometers

To make your temperature and humidity observations, you will need:
A U-shaped maximum/minimum thermometer, mounted on a board, with a magnet attached. (You can buy inexpensive thermometers at gardening shops and department stores.)
An ordinary thermometer (also mounted on a board)
A yogurt container

Distilled or boiled water
A strip of cheesecloth or muslin
Thumbtacks
A set of hygrometric tables. (You can find these in a book – *Smithsonian Meteorological Tables*, by Robert J. List, available at your public library.)
An electric drill
A screwdriver
Two plastic anchors
Two screws

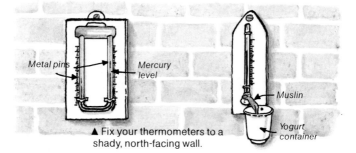

Metal pins

Mercury level

Muslin

Yogurt container

▲ Fix your thermometers to a shady, north-facing wall.

There is a metal pin in each arm of the U-shaped thermometer. The left-hand one records maximum temperatures, the right-hand one minimum temperatures. The mercury level in each arm shows actual air temperature. Note the actual temperature two or three times a day, and maximum and minimum temperatures for one day and night on the next morning.

Reset the thermometer by drawing the metal pins down with the magnet, so that they rest on top of the mercury.

The maximum/minimum thermometer will give you ordinary air temperature readings, so you only need a wet bulb thermometer to complete your hygrometer.

Pin the yogurt container to the base of the board behind the ordinary thermometer, and half fill it with water. Then wind the strip of cheesecloth around the bulb of the thermometer, leaving one end trailing in the water.

Make wet bulb readings when you make ordinary air temperature readings. Notice the difference between them, then work out the relative humidity using the hygrometric tables.

Fix the thermometers to a north-facing wall. Ask an adult to drill two holes in the wall, then fix in the plastic anchors and the screws and hang the thermometers from the screws.

Rain gauge

Rain gauges measure the depth of rain or snow which would cover the ground if none of it drained away or evaporated. To make one, you will need:

A flat-bottomed glass bottle
A plastic funnel with the same diameter as the bottle. (If necessary, buy a larger funnel and cut it to fit.)
A tall, narrow, glass jar
Masking tape
A pen
A ruler
A shovel

Collecting bottle

Tape marked in inches

Measuring jar

▲ To get precise readings, use a very narrow measuring jar.

Funnel

Same diameter

▲ Place the rain gauge away from trees (they may drip water into it).

Mark off a strip of tape in inches and stick it to the side of the bottle. Pour water into the bottle until it reaches the one inch mark. Then stick a strip of tape to the jar; tip the water out of the bottle into the jar and mark the level it reaches on the tape. Do the same for two inches, three and so on until the scale on the jar goes up to ten inches.

Put the funnel in the neck of the bottle, then dig a hole in the ground deep enough to hold the rain gauge.

Every morning, tip the rain collected in the bottle during the previous 24 hours into the jar to measure it. If the amount is too small to measure, it is called a "trace".

Melt snow before you pour it into the measuring jar. Ten inches of dry, powdery snow melts into about one inch of water. You can also measure snow simply by sticking a ruler into it.

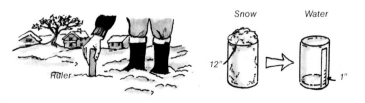

Ruler

Snow   Water

12"   1"

Wind sock

Wind socks act as anemometers and wind vanes combined. To make one, you will need:
One square yard of lightweight cloth
A wire coathanger
A curtain ring
A garden stake about 2 feet long
A needle and thread
Scissors
Strong string or rope
A broomstick
Cardboard
A compass
Clear tape
Colored paper
Thumbtacks

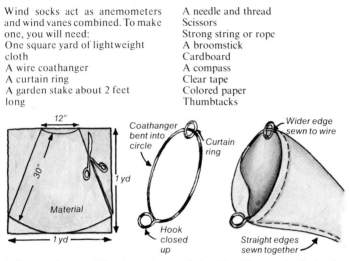

1. Cut out the material and sew the straight edges together.
2. Bend the coathanger into a circle, then squeeze the hook closed, so that it forms a small ring.
3. Slip the curtain ring onto the wire circle at the side opposite the hook. Then sew the wide, curved edge of the material onto the wire circle, leaving the hook and the curtain ring sticking out.

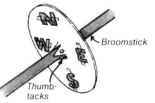

4. Cut out a circle of cardboard about 12 inches in diameter. Make two crossing slits in the center of the cardboard circle. Each slit should be about the same length as the diameter of the broomstick. Then cut the letters N, E, S, and W out of the colored paper and tape them to one side of the cardboard circle, to act as points of the compass.
5. Slide the cardboard circle over the broomstick and pin the slitted edges to the broomstick.

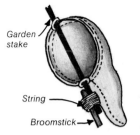

Garden stake

String

Broomstick

Compass

6. Tie the garden stake and the broomstick together, holding the broomstick with the compass points on the underside of the cardboard (so that you will be able to see them from below). Wind lots of string around the top of the

broomstick to keep the wire circle from sliding down.

7. Go outside and find north, using the compass. Before you set up your wind sock, make sure the N on the cardboard is pointing to north.

Wind

Clothes line post

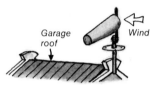

Garage roof

Wind

8. Set up the wind sock well away from anything that might stop the wind from blowing freely (trees, buildings or fences). It should be about 30 feet above ground level, but 6 feet or more will do. Tie the

broomstick to a clothes line post or fence or ask an adult to nail it to a shed or garage roof for you. The wind sock will turn to face the direction the wind is coming from.

Hurricane force   30 knots

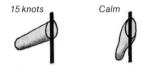

15 knots   Calm

The pictures above are a rough guide for judging wind speed from the angle of the wind sock. You can work out an accurate scale by asking an adult to drive you along a quiet road on a calm day. Hold the wind sock out of the car window and note the angle it blows at at different speeds. You can leave the scale in miles or kilometers per hour, or convert it into knots.

Make observations of wind speed and direction two or three times a day. The wind may blow in gusts. For example, the average wind speed may be 15 knots, occasionally reaching 20 knots. You would then write down wind speed as 15 knots, and add "gusting to 20 knots".

Visibility

Weather forecasters think of visibility as the furthest distance at which an object can be clearly seen. For example, when an object a mile away can be seen, but an object five miles away cannot, visibility is poor.

Distance	Visibility
200 yards	fog
1000 yards	mist or haze
1 mile	poor
5 miles	moderate
over 5 miles	good

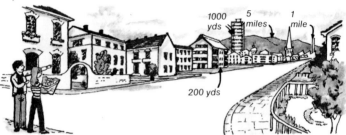

To make your own visibility scale, you will need a survey map of your area, a pen and paper.

On a clear day, go outside, or to an upstairs window (wherever you can get a good view) and pick out six objects and landmarks you can see, all different distances away. Use the map to work out how far away each one is, then write out a scale like the one above.

Make visibility observations two or three times a day.

Keeping a log book

You can enter your observations in a log book. Use a large exercise book or a file. It's a good idea to add remarks describing each day as well.

Date	Time	Pressure		Wind		Cloud	Visibility	Humidity
		Mb	trend	speed (knots)	direction	cover (oktas)	(miles)	(%)
June 3rd 1990	8am	30.2	⌐	10	SW	4	4	60
	1pm	30.1	\	15	SW	8	1	90
	6pm	30.1	∨	15	W	1	9	50

Keeping a scrapbook

You can record the weather in maps and pictures as well as by writing observations in your log book.

When something interesting connected with the weather happens in your area, like a fall of huge hailstones, floods after heavy rains, hurricane force winds, a freak heatwave, blizzards or even a tornado, cut out any pictures of the event from the newspaper and paste them in a scrapbook along with the weather map for that day. Write the date at the top of the page. You can paste your own photographs in too.

Taking photographs

Sunrise   Mid-day   6 p.m.

To make a cloud chart, you can take photographs of different clouds and paste them in your scrapbook, labeling each one. Or try recording a whole day by taking a photograph every hour or two, starting at sunrise and ending at sunset.

If you take photographs of the same cloud (a large cumulus is best) at five-minute intervals, you will see how fast it changes.

If you can't make observations three times a day, just make them in the morning and evening. Try to find someone to do them for you if you go away.

Temperature (°F)	Maximum Temperature	Minimum Temperature	Precipitation (ins)	Remarks
47	52	39	$\frac{1}{4}$	mild, cloudy morning
50				heavy rain at midday
43				clear, dry evening

Weather lore

There are many traditional sayings about the weather. Your weather observations should help you decide which ones are reliable aids to forecasting. Here are some examples:

"Mackerel sky and mares' tails Make tall ships carry low sails."
Cirrus and cirrocumulus are early warning signs of rain and wind coming on the warm front of a depression.

"The bigger the ring, The nearer the rain."
Haloes around the sun or moon are made by light shining through cirrostratus, another early warning sign of a warm front.

"Rain before seven, Fine before eleven."
Belts of rain brought by fronts tend to last less than six hours. However, this saying is true of rain at any time, not just before seven.

"Fast runs the ant As the mercury rises."
Ants are natural barometers. They run faster in warm weather when pressure is high, or rising, than in cool, low pressure weather.

"Red sky at night, shepherds delight, Red sky in the morning, sailors take warning."
Red skies happen in dry air full of dust. A red western sky in the evening can mean a dry day ahead.

Weather moves from west to east as a rule. Similarly, a red morning sky lighting up a layer of clouds can mean there is some rain or snow on the way.

Going further

Any weather station will be glad to supply you with a lot of helpful information. The National Weather Service (US) is listed in the telephone book under US Government, Department of Commerce, NOAA.

There are offices all over the United States. The Atmospheric Environment Service (Canada) is listed in the telephone book under government addresses for each province.

Books to read

Pocket Weather Forecaster. (Barrons). *The Weather Almanac.* James Ruffner and Frank Bair (eds), (Avon).
Weather. Paul Lehr, R. W. Burnett & H. Zim (Golden Press).

Instant Weather Forecasting. Alan Watts (Dodd, Mead).
Weather Wisdom. Albert Lee (Doubleday/Dolphin).
Eric Sloane's Almanac and Weather Forecaster. (Hawthorne).

Index